TOLONO PUBLIC LIBRARY
W9-BNU-742

FIGMENT 2
THE LEGACY OF IMAGINATION: VOLUME 1
ABDO Spotlight
Disney KINGDOMS
MARVEL

ABDOPUBLISHING.COM

Reinforced library bound edition published in 2017 by Spotlight,
a division of ABDO, PO Box 398166, Minneapolis, Minnesota 55439.
Spotlight produces high-quality reinforced library bound editions for
schools and libraries. Published by agreement with Marvel Characters, Inc.

Printed in the United States of America, North Mankato, Minnesota.
092016
012017

PUBLISHER'S CATALOGING IN PUBLICATION DATA

Names: Zub, Jim, author. | Bachs, Ramon ; Beaulieu, Jean-Francois, illustrators.
Title: Figment 2 : The Legacy of Imagination / writer: Jim Zub ; art: Ramon Bachs ; Jean-Francois Beaulieu.
Description: Reinforced library bound edition. | Minneapolis, Minnesota : Spotlight, 2017. | Series: Disney Kingdoms : Figment Set 2
Summary: After flying through a portal, Dreamfinder and Figment find themselves in the 21st century at the new Academy, but when a demonstration goes wrong, Dreamfinder transforms into the Doubtfinder, leaving Figment and Capri to free Dreamfinder before doubt can take over the world.
Identifiers: LCCN 2016941716 | ISBN 9781614795810 (volume 1) | ISBN 9781614795827 (volume 2) | ISBN 9781614795834 (volume 3) | ISBN 9781614795841 (volume 4) | ISBN 9781614795858 (volume 5)
Subjects: LCSH: Disney (Fictitious characters)--Juvenile fiction. | Adventure and adventurers--Juvenile fiction. | Comic books, strips, etc.--Juvenile fiction. | Graphic novels--Juvenile fiction.
Classification: DDC 741.5--dc23
LC record available at https://lccn.loc.gov/2016941716

Spotlight

A Division of ABDO
abdopublishing.com

Early Figment and Dreamfinder character designs for the Journey Into Imagination ride by X Atencio

Artwork courtesy of Walt Disney Imagineering Art Collection

Imagination. Such a wonderful application of the human mind – to conjure up dreams and use them to better the world. Blarion Mercurial, a young inventor at the Academy Scientifica-Lucidus, did literally that when he created **Figment** using his newly designed, thought-powered machine. Soon after, the machine pulled them both into a dreamlike world where they visited fantastic realms of pure imagination, and made new friends along the way, before Blair eventually reached his full creative potential and emerged transformed as the **Dreamfinder.**

Dreamfinder and Figment found themselves back on Earth in time to save the planet from a destructive force unleashed by his own invention. In taking down the threat, the duo piloted their flying Dream Machine through a portal to a place truly beyond imagination: modern-day Earth.

Florida, USA.
Now.
Looks like you've got another one, Jess.
Thanks, Bill.
That girl of yours, she's just living up to her name. She can't help it.
I know...
sigh
CAPRICIOUS HARMONY
INDIAN RIVER DRIVE
COCOA, FLORIDA
USA
Capri...
CAPRI!
Thump, whump, bam bam bam!
Coming!

Did they send a reply?!
DID I GET IN?!
Capricious Aloysia Harmony... you're a complete wreck.
Look what you've done to your favorite dress...
A worthy sacrifice in the name of science, Mom, but there's no time for that! Just gimme the letter!
"Dear Ms. Harmony...
"Thank you for your enthusiastic thesis submission and subsequent repeated correspondence about your current application status...
"All of us at Academy Scientifica-Lucidus USA acknowledge and appreciate your family's connection to our esteemed institution...
"...but due to academic requirements we cannot offer you a seat in our Invention & Ingenuity program until you reach physical maturity..."
I'm sorry, honey.
I know you worked really hard on this, but it's not the right time.
Yeah...
No matter what that letter says, I don't want you to give up hope...

"...your dreams will come true some day."
Look, Figment...
...a brand-new place full of wonderful curiosities to uncover!
Wowie-WOW, Dreamfinder. I can't wait!
SPUTTER
Uh-oh... I think our Dream Machine is all tuckered out.
PUTT PUTT PUTT
That seems like a good landing spot.

It's time to explore!
Wheee!

The Legacy Of Imagination

Part One: Living Legends

JIM ZUB writer
RAMON BACHS artist
JEAN-FRANCOIS BEAULIEU colorist
VC's JOE CARAMAGNA letterer

JOHN TYLER CHRISTOPHER cover artist
X ATENCIO Imagineer variant cover artist
JOHN TYLER CHRISTOPHER action figure variant cover

ANDY DIGENOVA, TOM MORRIS, & JOSH SHIPLEY
Walt Disney Imagineers

EMILY SHAW consulting editor
MARK BASSO editor

AXEL ALONSO editor in chief **JOE QUESADA** chief creative officer
DAN BUCKLEY publisher

Special Thanks to **DAVID GABRIEL & BRIAN CROSBY**

SHAKE
tkka tkka tkka
WOOSH!
That's not good...
ahem
Greetings, everyone!
You may call me Dreamfinder, and this is Figment!
Hello, hello, hello!
Whoa!
Crazy cosplay!
Are you seeing this?
What... what is that? A light box?
Wh-wh-what is the meaning of this?!
Is this some kind of prank?!
No prank, my good man, it's a profession!
Though we're not paid very well for it...
Are you serious? Dude, it's a smart phone.
That's a PHONE?
My flying friend and I are here to--
Uh...
I don't believe it--

This...
This is the Academy!
ACADEMY SCIENTIFICA-LUCIDUS EST. 1881
Of course it's the Academy, you barmy buffoon!
It's also private property!
You can't just use our courtyard as your own personal landing strip or waltz around dressed like that! We have rules!
After all this time, back at the Academy...
It's destiny!
HEY! Are you even listening to me?!
It looks different!
I hope they didn't sell your stuff... you had lots of books I wanted to read!
Oh, WOW!

BLARION MERCURIAL
1882-1910
"A DREAM CAN BE A DREAM COME TRUE."
Can I *help* you?
Are you looking for someone in *particular?*
I...
As I was saying, this little *practical joke* has gone *far enough!*
It's *no joke,* good sir...
That... that's *me!*
This is *Figment!* And I am...or was...*Blair Mercurial!*
He *is!* We *are!*
We traveled here through the *Realms of Imagination!*

Stop playing around! It's not funny!
I'm not! I'm serious!
Yo, Figment. Take a photo, quick!
Those little light boxes... how does that even work? Where are the gears?!
Everyone's so excited! Are we all friends now?
Stay calm, everybody.
Chairman Auckley, what's the problem here?
This crazy man and his pet... whatever that is... they've parked a vehicle on the lawn and they're disrupting the start of classes!
Is this true? The vehicle and the whatnot?
Yes, but not the way he's saying it. Figment and I were brought here by dream power. This is where we're meant to be!
See? He's impersonating esteemed faculty and trespassing to boot.
Escort them off the grounds and impound that contraption!
I'm sure we can work this all out. We don't mean any harm.
Uh...
Figment's right. I'm sure this all just a misunderstanding. We just need someone to verify our identities and then--
BLAIR! FIGMENT!

Is it really you, after all these years?
FYE!
Our friend and fellow traveler!
Astonishing!
You... you look so different! How long have we been away?
Over a hundred years, my friend.
A hundred years since Chairman Illocrant and I watched you two banish the Articulate Army and save London.*
A hundred years since your journey into imagination.
*See the original FIGMENT miniseries. --Mark
A century gone but we've kept the Academy running, my friend...
Generations of students have been eager to follow in your footsteps.
I...I'm so glad you're here to see it.
YAAAAAY!

You're telling me this is the Blair Mercurial? You're sure?!
One hundred percent sure, Chairman.
We're the genuine article, your Chairfullness.
I always assumed the little dragon on the statue was just imaginary...
I am, but that doesn't mean I'm not real.
Right...
chairman auckley
Where are we? What happened to the hustle and bustle of London?
A few years after you vanished, old man Illocrant decided the best way to avoid a lawsuit was to find a secluded space where we could conduct our experiments in peace.
He bought a big plot of land in Florida and built a whole new Academy here.
Chairman Illocrant, Chairman Porter, Chairman LeFoof, and now me... Chairman Auckley.
A tradition of inventive excellence here at Scientifica-Lucidus. One I'm proud to uphold.
I must admit I'm finding this hard to believe, though I can't deny that it's nice to see Mr. Fye so happy.
I'll show you around, then we'll discuss your possible future here at the Academy.
Yippee!

Down that hall is Professor Brainard's lab. He's visiting from Medfield...
This is our Invention & Ingenuity department, where new students begin their studies.
A school of discovery, an institute of imagination! Boy oh boy, when can I start?
We're already midway through the semester, Figment. Maybe next term?
We have strict rules for applicants, Mr. Figment. Maybe once you reach adulthood and pass our entry requirements...
I'm sure an exception could be made for--
No exceptions!
A place like this can't function if everyone runs around breaking the rules, doing whatever they want!
I don't understand...
And that is why you can't be a student!
Is he always like this?
He's not a bad guy... he's just a bit, y'know, rigid.
This way! Lots more to see!

This is our latest experiment. These containers will house stored up energy from our new generator.
Where are the valves and pistons? I don't recognize any of this.
Is there a power source?
Welcome to the 21st century, Mr. Mercurial...
Well, that's part of the problem. Come this way...
The potential source...is that!
Oh, I see! I wondered what that was.
I'm wondering now! So, what is it?
Hmmm...
That's just it! We don't even know!
That giant geodesic sphere appeared over thirty years ago and no one knows what it is or how it got here.
Sometimes it'll vanish for a few months at a time, but it always comes back, sitting right there, defying explanation.
Our sensors detect a great deal of energy within.
Yes, and we need to harness it soon to keep the Academy running. At our current rate of consumption, we'll run out of juice in a few weeks!
If you're looking for energy, there's nothing better than dream power.
He's right! I'm living proof!
I've perused the reports on your adventures written by Mr. Fye and Chairman Illocrant, but I must say they read more like fiction than fact...
Just watch what they can do, Chairman. Then you'll believe as I do.

This, my friends, is the Dream Machine!
Blair summoned it from his mind and powered it with imagination!
I don't doubt your excitement, but it just looks like an eccentric dirigible. The technology is archaic at best.
That means it's a "classic," right?
Not quite...
SHAKA-SHAKA-SHAKA-SHAKA-
CLICKETY-CLICK
This old flyer's been with us through a lot.
It's no longer in pristine condition, but it's got it where it counts.
SHAKA-SHAKA-SHAKA-SHAKA
Watch, watch!
Oh, I'm watching, I assure you...
FOOOOM!
WHOA!

FOO-
Thump Thump
SCRAAAAAPE!
FOO-
FOOOOM!
Don't WORRY! I've GOT this!
Oh no...
I think that's a new feature...
C'mon...
KER-CHAK!
WHOOSH!
Ah-HA!

VOOOM!
Careful now!
This is madness!
DREAMFINDER!
Urk!
SMASH!

BOOOM!
Abandon ship!
KER-RAASH!
Never fear, Figment's here!

FWIP-FWIP-FWIP
Think light thoughts!
light thoughts-light thoughts-light thoughts!
WHUMP!
"Dream energy," eh?
I think not!
PIFF
PIFF
PIFF
PIFF
I'm sure they're just--
Enough.
Our Academy is in a time of crisis and that foolish flyer could have damaged our new power source!
For years I'd heard tales of the "brilliant Dreamfinder" but he's anything but!
Ridiculous, reckless, and hopelessly out of touch!
Get this junk off the lawn and leave me to my work!

I know that didn't go as planned, but we'll let it lie for now. You two can impress the whole Academy with dream power tomorrow, okay?
Yeah. Sure...
Just stay here. I'll go get the janitor to collect up the machine bits in the yard so we can put it back together.
Okey-dokey.
No gears or pistons... everything's so different, Figment.
How did this happen? What about the power of imagination?
It just... it didn't work...
When we saved London I felt like I could do anything.
I imagined things and in a flash they came true.
But now, instead of believing, I just... I froze up.
I had that awful feeling all over again.
That feeling I had before I succeeded with the Mesmonic Converter.
"Feeling"?
What feeling?

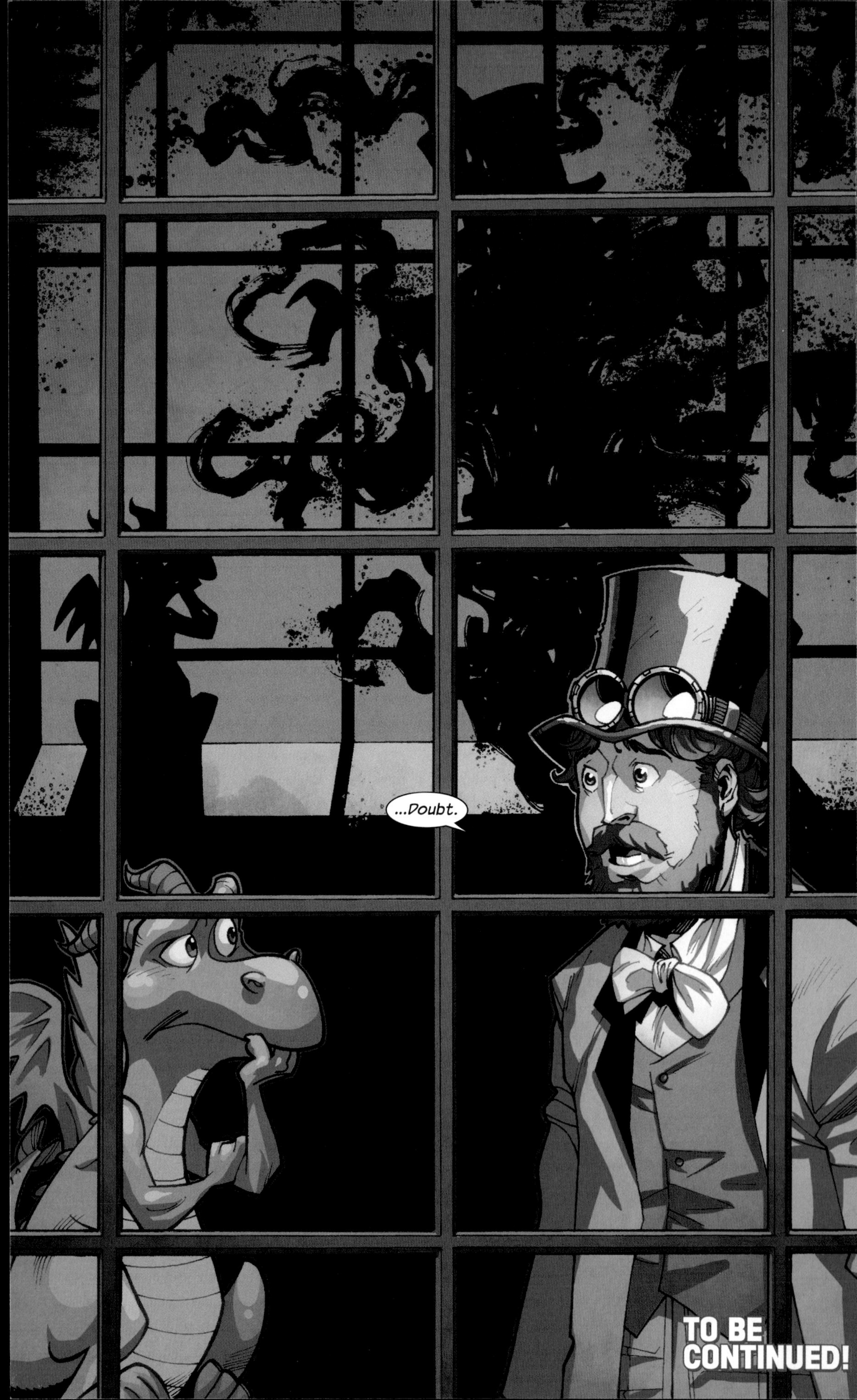
...Doubt.
TO BE CONTINUED!